Jill Bryant

Contents

Volcanic Vents

A volcano is an opening, or **vent**, that extends from the surface of Earth down through its crust. During a volcanic **eruption**, hot material gushes out of the vent, including melted rock, chunks of solid rock, gas and ash.

Volcanic ash is made up of crushed particles of rock, other minerals and fragments of volcanic glass. When a volcano erupts, a stream of ash and rock can shoot more than 30 kilometres into the air. This forms a tall column called an ash plume.

The hot, liquid rock that oozes below Earth's surface is called magma. Once it bursts through the vent and pours outside onto the ground, it is known as lava. Cooled lava hardens to form rock such as pumice or obsidian.

Volcán de Fuego, Guatemala, is a type of volcano known as a volcanic peak.

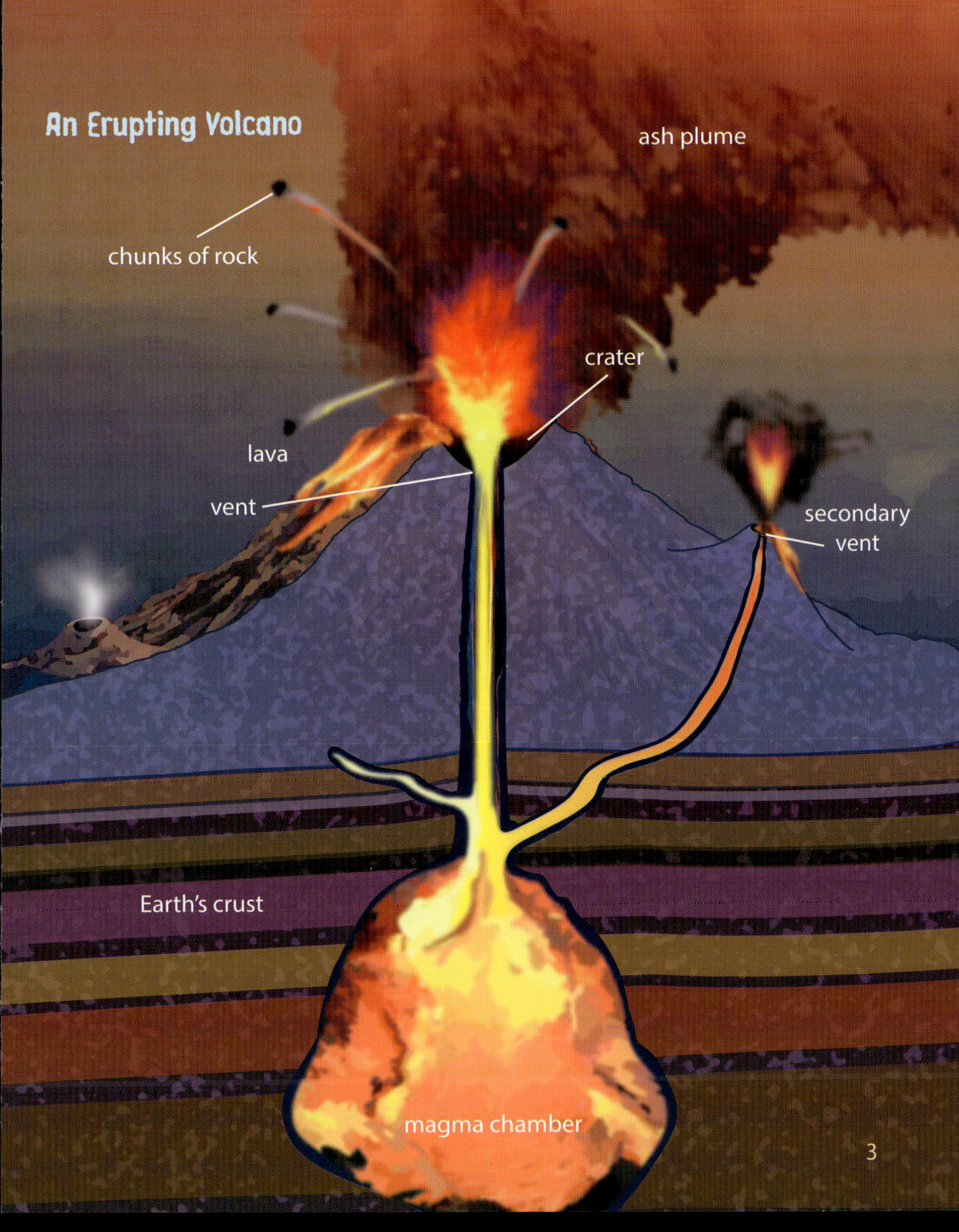
An Erupting Volcano
ash plume
chunks of rock
crater
lava
vent
secondary vent
Earth's crust
magma chamber

Volcanoes on Land and at Sea

Each time volcanoes erupt, they change the landscape. Massive eruptions leave behind large holes that become valleys. Lava flows over the surface, creating distinctive rock formations as it hardens. Some volcanic eruptions can even create new islands at sea.

THINK AND TALK ABOUT ...
It can take days, months or years for hot liquid lava to cool completely and harden into rock.

Cold lava becomes rock.

Devil's Tower, USA, is a famous volcanic neck.

Peaks, Calderas and Necks

The most common shape for a volcano is a steep-sided cone with a **crater** at the top. This shape is known as a volcanic peak.

After a massive eruption, the top of the cone collapses, due to the ejection of the magma that was underneath the mountain. This can form an uneven, vast hole called a **caldera**. Calderas are more than a kilometre wide. Sometimes, they fill with rain to form deep lakes.

Sometimes, a column of hardened magma is trapped inside the vent during the eruption. This is called a volcanic neck. The rock in volcanic necks is much harder than the rock on the outside of the mountain, so it doesn't erode at the same rate as the rest of the old volcano. Frequently, the volcanic neck is the last part of a peak to remain.

Seamounts

Often, volcanoes form under the water. They are called seamounts. Like volcanoes on land, when seamounts erupt, lava pours out. As the lava cools into rock under the water, it creates volcanic mountains with high peaks. Some seamounts grow tall enough that they break through the ocean's surface, and their peaks become volcanic islands.

Seamounts that do not break the surface can be thousands of metres under the water and very far from any shore. It is not always possible to know that they have erupted. Scientists believe that most volcanic eruptions on Earth occur in the ocean. The water around the vent fills with bubbles as gas begins to erupt from the volcano. During an underwater eruption, the ocean can become hot and there can be a lot of waves on the surface.

A plume of ash erupts from a seamount deep under the ocean.

THINK AND TALK ABOUT ...

Chains of deep-sea volcanoes can create extreme, hot-water environments that are home to many rare sea creatures, such as tube worms.

Plates and Hotspots

Most volcanoes are located along the boundaries between the **tectonic plates** that cover Earth. These huge plates can shift and slide, causing extreme events on the surface above, such as earthquakes, tsunamis and volcanic eruptions.

Some volcanoes occur at other parts of a tectonic plate, in places called hotspots. Hotspots are regions in Earth's mantle in which rock melts and becomes magma. This wells upwards. As tectonic plates slowly move, different parts of Earth's crust pass over the hotspot. This can cause a chain of volcanoes. If these volcanoes are tall enough to break the surface, they become a chain of islands. There are hotspot volcanoes in Hawaii, Iceland, the Galápagos Islands and other places.

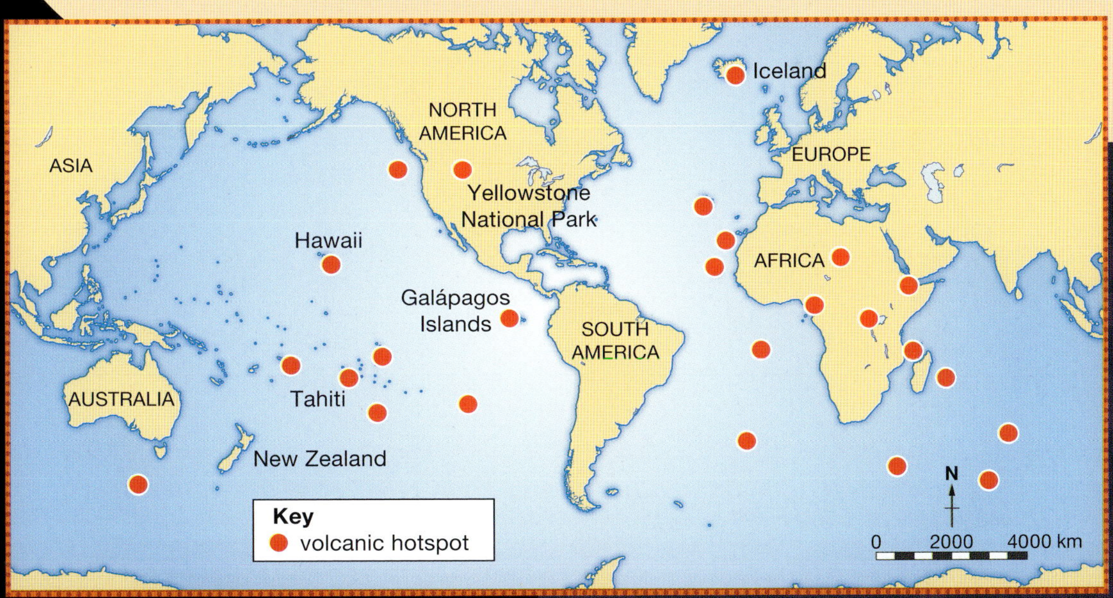

major volcanic hotspots of the world

Active and Extinct Volcanoes

There are about 40 000 volcanoes on Earth, but some have not erupted in millions of years. A volcano that has erupted at least once in the last 10 000 years is called an active volcano.

Active volcanoes can be either erupting or **dormant**. Every day, between 10 and 20 active volcanoes erupt. A dormant volcano is an active volcano that is not erupting now, but is expected to erupt again.

An extinct volcano is one that has not erupted in 10 000 years or more. Scientists think that most of these volcanoes have been cut off from their source of magma, and cannot ever erupt again.

The city of Auckland, New Zealand, developed around the crater of the extinct volcano Mount Eden.

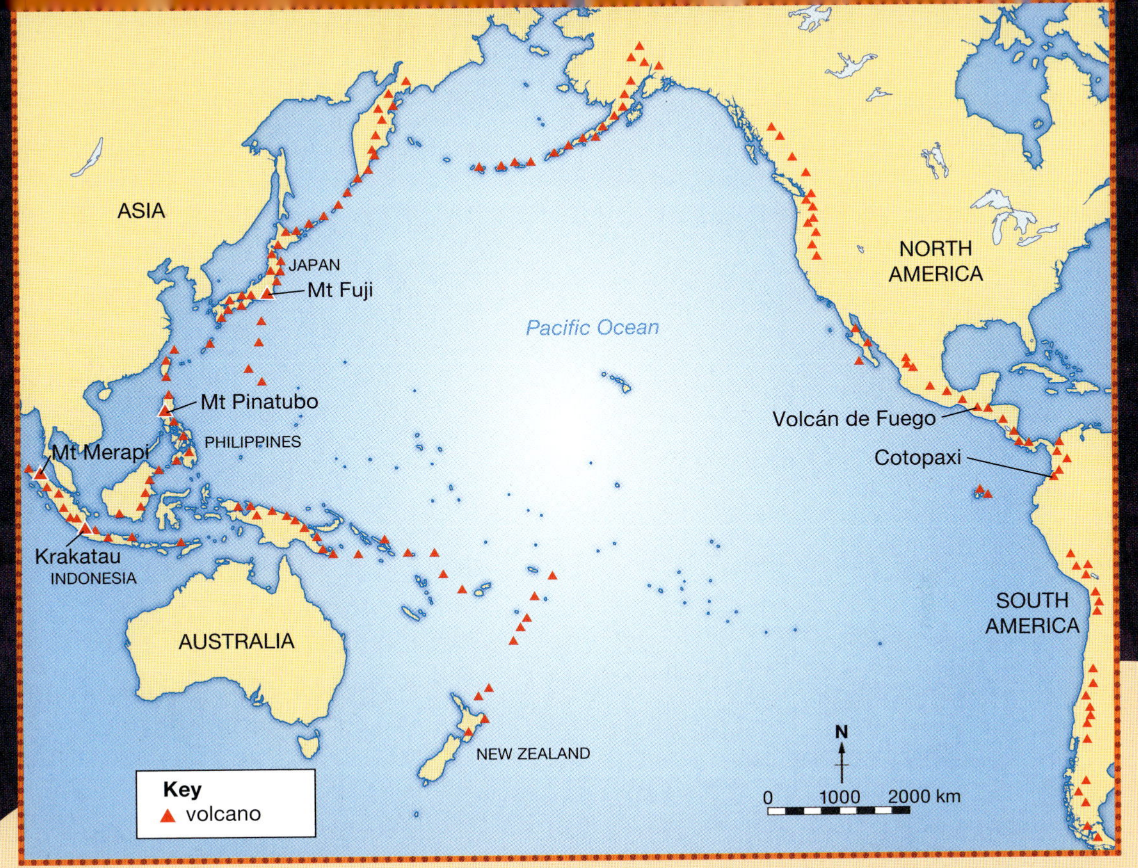

The many volcanoes around the shoreline of the Pacific Ocean form the Ring of Fire.

The Ring of Fire

An upside-down U-shaped string of volcanoes follows the shoreline of the Pacific Ocean. This area is called the Ring of Fire. Scientists think that 75 per cent of all active volcanoes are in the Ring of Fire.

The volcanoes of the Ring of Fire have formed due to the movement of tectonic plates. When the huge, heavy Pacific plate bumps up against smaller, lighter plates, it causes magma to rise up and volcanoes to erupt. Japan, Indonesia and the Andes Mountains in South America are all part of the Ring of Fire, with many active volcanoes.

Andes Mountains

There is a chain of volcanoes along the west coast of South America. Many parts of the region are **remote**: the mountains are high and few people live close by. Therefore, even today it is possible for volcanoes in the Andes Mountains to erupt without anyone knowing it has happened.

Japan

There are 110 active volcanoes in Japan, on the land and in the sea. Some of Japan's islands were created by volcanic eruptions. When volcanoes threaten to erupt in Japan, often hundreds of thousands of people must leave their homes until the danger passes.

Indonesia

Indonesia has 129 active volcanoes. Many volcanic eruptions have occurred in the past 100 years. With people scattered across more than 6000 small islands, it is sometimes difficult for people in Indonesia to flee to safety when a volcano threatens to erupt.

Hawaii

Hawaii, in the middle of the Pacific Ocean, is encircled by the Ring of Fire, even though it is not part of it. The islands of Hawaii are made from hotspot volcanoes that have erupted so many times that the hardened lava reaches above the surface of the sea. Beyond the islands, seamounts continue beneath the water for 3000 kilometres.

Cotopaxi is an active volcano in the Andes Mountains, Ecuador.

Mount Fuji, Japan, last erupted more than 300 years ago.

THINK AND TALK ABOUT ...

Mount Fuji has inspired many artists. It is featured in the famous print *The Great Wave off Kanagawa* by the artist Hokusai.

Other Regions with Active Volcanoes

Iceland

Iceland has approximately 130 volcanoes, 30 to 40 of which are active. Iceland is located between two tectonic plates. These plates are drifting apart, which causes magma to rise up in the gap. Iceland is also on top of a hotspot, which attracts more magma to the surface. Iceland usually has a major volcanic eruption every four or five years.

The Mediterranean

There are nearly 50 volcanoes in the Mediterranean region in Europe. Most volcanoes in the Mediterranean are on islands or on the coast of the **mainland**. Greece and Italy have a long history of volcanic eruptions. Mount Etna in Rome, Italy, is considered by many to be the most active volcano in Europe. Records about Mount Etna erupting go back almost 2500 years.

the 2010 eruption of Eyjafjallajokull, Iceland

Mount Etna, Italy, erupting in 2015

Great Rift Valley, Kenya

Great Rift Valley

The deep, flat-bottomed Great Rift Valley is another volcano-rich region. It begins at the Mediterranean Sea and continues through most of East Africa. The valley is so vast it can be seen from space. The East African countries of Ethiopia, Kenya, Uganda and Tanzania host many of the valley's 30 active volcanoes.

THINK AND TALK ABOUT ...

After large volcanic eruptions, ash in the atmosphere affects visibility and can lead to cancelled flights. In 2015, travellers to Bali were stranded after the explosion of Mount Ruang in East Java, Indonesia.

Looking Way Back

Ontong Java Plateau

About 125 million years ago, when dinosaurs shared Earth with the first birds, a massive eruption created a vast **plateau** in the South Pacific Ocean, known as the Ontong Java Plateau. This mostly submerged plateau is about 2 million square kilometres in area, which is roughly the size of Mexico. The eruption is said to have produced a million times more lava than the largest eruption recorded by humans in the past 2500 years.

Deccan Traps

The distinctive rock formations of Deccan Traps, India, were created by a series of volcanoes that exploded about 66 million years ago. The gigantic eruptions covered the land, plants and animals in lava for 500 000 square kilometres. The eruptions also poisoned the air with **toxic** gases. Many scientists believe these gases may have created changes in Earth's climate that contributed to the extinction of the dinosaurs.

Old lava flows created strange rock formations at Deccan Traps.

The magma below Yellowstone National Park creates hot springs.

Yellowstone

The volcano at Yellowstone National Park, USA, is classified as a supervolcano, due to the massive power of its eruptions. The last time the Yellowstone supervolcano fully exploded was 640 000 years ago. The supervolcano had some smaller eruptions about 70 000 years ago, which were still major eruptions by the standards of more recent history. Nicknamed the "Sleeping Giant", the Yellowstone supervolcano has the potential to bury most of the USA and part of Canada in ash, if it has another massive eruption.

Famous Volcanoes

Around the world, there are volcanoes that are particularly famous or important to the people living near them. This can be because of their strange shape, their record-breaking size and devastating eruptions, or because they have an interesting past. Mount Fuji, Mount Etna and the Yellowstone supervolcano are all famous volcanoes, but there are others.

Spotlight on Italy

Vulcano

The island of Vulcano was named after the ancient Roman god Vulcan. Vulcan was said to use fire to forge weapons with divine qualities. The English word "volcano" also comes from Vulcan's name. Today, tourists travel by boat to visit Vulcano's black sand beach, hot mud baths and the hiking trails up its two volcanic craters.

the island of Vulcano, Italy

Mount Vesuvius can be seen behind the ruins of Pompeii.

This mosaic was uncovered in the ruins of Pompeii.

Mount Vesuvius

Located near the modern-day city of Naples, Mount Vesuvius is best known for burying the ancient city of Pompeii, in 79 CE. When the residents of Pompeii observed the first warning signs from the volcano, many fled the city by boat. Of the 2000 people who remained, none could escape the hot lava and ash racing down the mountainside at 112 kilometres per hour. Mount Vesuvius's most recent eruption was in 1944.

Spotlight on Hawaii

Kilauea

Five volcanoes make up the main island of Hawaii. The three most famous are Kilauea, Mauna Kea and Mauna Loa. Kilauea is currently the most active volcano in the world. It has been erupting continuously since 1983. About 200 homes have been destroyed by the molten lava. During the day, a rising column of gas can be seen. After dark, the lava lake inside the crater **emits** a fiery glow.

Mauna Kea

When it is measured from its base deep under the sea, Mauna Kea is the tallest mountain in the world. At 10 205 metres, it is actually 40 metres taller than Mount Everest, the world's highest peak. Only 4205 metres of Mauna Kea are above sea level, however, with another 6000 metres under the water. Mauna Kea is a dormant volcano.

Mauna Loa

Mauna Loa is the largest volcano on Earth. At its widest point, it measures 120 kilometres across. It covers more than half of the main island of Hawaii. Mauna Loa is an active volcano. It has erupted 33 times in the past 200 years.

Lava fills one of Kilauea's vents.

Spotlight on Indonesia

Mount Merapi

Mount Merapi is the most active volcano in Indonesia. It erupts every five to ten years, and produces a near-steady stream of lava. More than one million people live near Mount Merapi, and hundreds of thousands of people must be **evacuated** whenever it starts to smoke and rumble. This includes thousands of farmers who live and grow crops on the mountainside.

Krakatau

The unoccupied island of Krakatau, sometimes called Krakatoa, is located between the large islands of Sumatra and Java. It used to be made up of three volcanic peaks. In May 1883, they began to eject ash, gas and rock. A few months later, all three peaks erupted, creating tsunamis that killed more than 36 000 people on the surrounding islands.

People as far away as Australia heard the explosion. It was the most powerful eruption ever recorded. Two thirds of the island were blasted apart. A new active volcano formed among the volcanic remains under the sea.

A new active volcano, Anak Krakatau, formed in the remains of Krakatau.

This drawing of the eruption of Krakatau was published in 1888.

Volcanologists

The study of rocks is called geology. Geologists who focus their research on volcanoes are called volcanologists. They are experts on volcanic processes, rocks, gases and chemical reactions.

Volcanologists can predict when a volcano will erupt. They raise the alarm when they observe these signs, and recommend evacuation orders be put into action. Warnings such as these can save many lives.

Volcanologists analyse rock samples and interpret data in laboratories, but many also travel to regions with volcanoes to study them. This can be both exciting and a little dangerous. Volcanologists often work in **hazardous** areas, close to active craters, where it is important to put safety first. Researchers usually work in pairs or small groups. They are trained in first aid, and know how to escape quickly, if it is necessary.

A volcanologist collects a sample of hot lava.

A Volcanologist's Protective Clothing and Gear

If they are working in an area where there are toxic gases and hot falling ash, volcanologists wear protective clothing.

Special Tools

Volcanologists use various instruments to collect data. A spectrometer analyses the light in a column of gas. The results help identify toxic gases. This tool is also useful for predicting eruptions.

Thermal images are photographs that use different colours to show how much heat is **radiating** from each area. These photos can be taken after an eruption to reveal which lava flows are still very hot and dangerous.

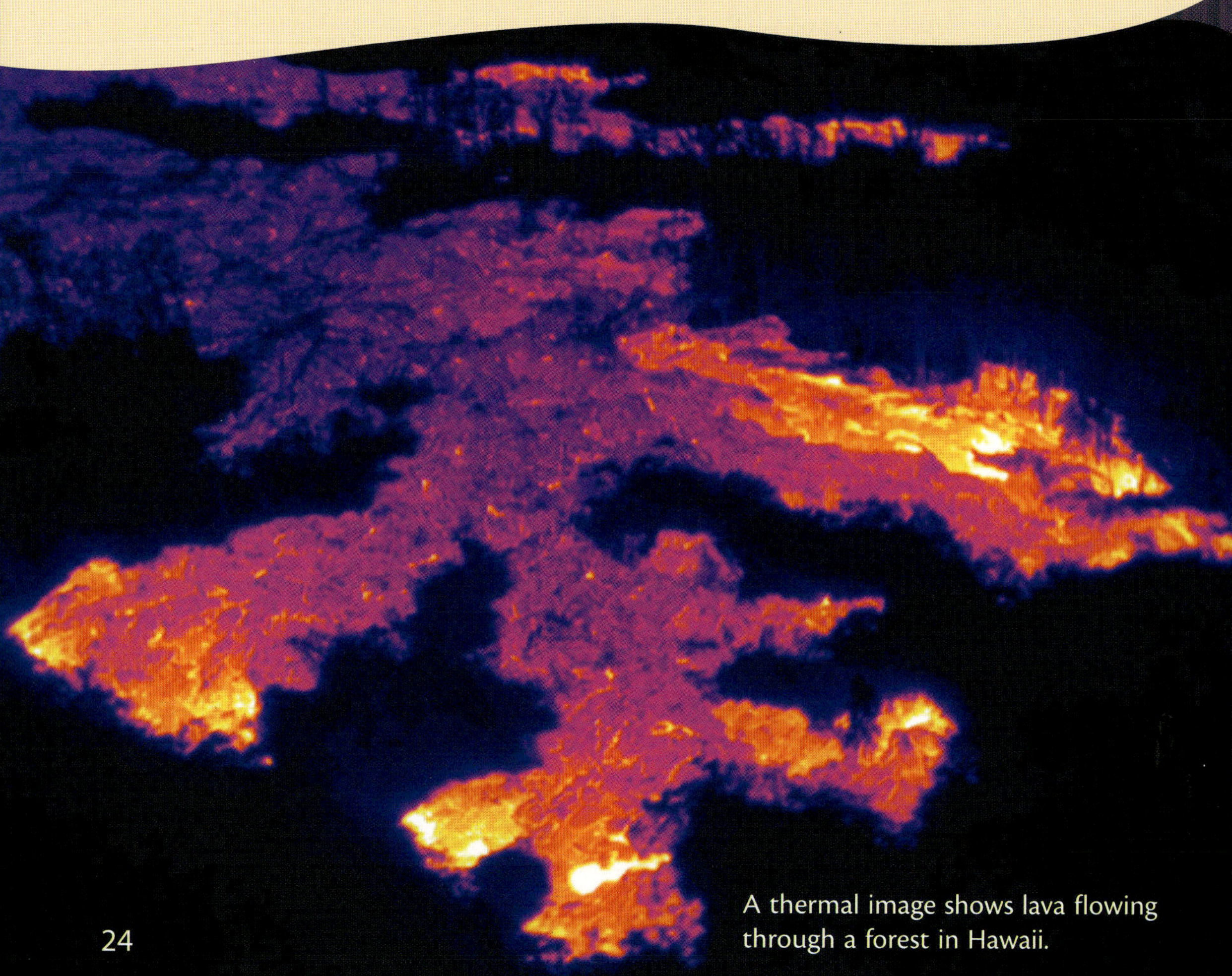

A thermal image shows lava flowing through a forest in Hawaii.

Sensors that detect movement in tectonic plates are known as **seismic** monitors. They are used primarily for predicting earthquakes, but their readings can also be used to predict volcanic eruptions.

Radar mapping equipment, on board satellites or aircraft, can be used to create three-dimensional maps. Knowing the exact shape of the land allows scientists to predict the paths of lava flows, which helps with planning evacuations.

A tiltmeter measures small changes in the shape of a volcano. Even a reading indicating the tiniest bulge can signal that magma is swelling beneath the sides of the mountain. This informs scientists that an eruption is likely to occur.

THINK AND TALK ABOUT ...

The scale for measuring volcanic explosions is called the Volcano Explosivity Index. The scale ranges from 0 (non-explosive) to 8 (mega-colossal).

Often, volcanologists need to collect data from a long way away, for safety.

Extreme Forces

Volcanoes are very interesting landforms to study and observe. When volcanic eruptions occur, they can destroy everything in their path. They are fiery, powerful and sometimes deadly.

Volcanic eruptions can create entirely new landscapes. Lakes and new islands owe their existence to volcanoes. Frequently, the caldera of a volcano becomes a rich and fertile area over time. Many dormant or extinct volcanoes have become popular sites for tourists and hikers.

Volcanoes also provide valuable scientific insights. Volcanic eruptions allow scientists to study molten rock and minerals from far beneath Earth's surface.

A lake has formed in Quilotoa caldera in the Andes Mountains, Ecuador.

MOUNT PINATUBO

Mount Pinatubo is a volcano in the Philippines. It is located in the Ring of Fire region, between two plate boundaries. It is surrounded by mountains.

Mount Pinatubo lay dormant for nearly 500 years. Thick rainforest covered its steep slopes. No one knew that it was becoming active until August 1990, when it blew out steam and began to rumble loudly. Volcanologists immediately started to watch the volcano closely.

In mid-March 1991, a series of tremors shook the area. On 2 April, a small explosion created a row of steaming vents along the mountain. This was followed by two months of billowing steam, shooting ash and deep rumblings.

Before the eruption, Aeta indigenous people farmed the land at the base of Mount Pinatubo.

On 5 June, volcanologists detected a bulge in the mountain that signalled that magma was swelling at the peak. They raised the alert and asked the 30 000 people who lived on and near the mountain to evacuate. Less than half did so. Mount Pinatubo had been dormant for so long that many people did not believe it could be dangerous.

On 7 June, an eruption created an ash plume that soared 8 kilometres into the air. After two days, the air was thick with the smell of sulphur. Hot gas and rock began to pour down the side of the mountain. Ash coated everything in a fine powder.

Officials insisted more people evacuate. People used umbrellas and scarves to shield themselves from the hot falling ash as they tried to leave the area. The highway filled with crowded vehicles bound for the city of Manila, 91 kilometres away.

Ash covers an evacuated village near Mount Pinatubo.

Mount Pinatubo's ash plume was more than 20 times higher than the peak itself.

For the next few days, particles of ash shot 25 kilometres into the air. Small earthquakes shook the area. The first violent eruption struck on 14 June, but it was on the following day, 15 June, that the main eruption hit.

First, a huge column of gas shot 34 kilometres into the air. Last-minute evacuations continued in pouring rain that turned the volcanic ash to thick, cement-like mud. Then, a devastating blast tore apart the rocky peak, reducing the height of Mount Pinatubo by 259 metres. It was the second-largest eruption of the twentieth century.

Ash from the eruption rose into the atmosphere and, over the next year, it spread around the world. The cloud of ash and toxic gases caused a global temperature drop of 0.5° C.

As a result of the eruption, hundreds of people lost their lives. But with so many people living nearby, the toll of the massive eruption could have been much worse. It was the careful monitoring and warnings of volcanologists that allowed so many people to be evacuated to safety in time.

A lake now fills the crater of Mount Pinatubo.

Glossary

caldera (*noun*)	the vast hole or valley left when a volcanic peak collapses after an eruption
crater (*noun*)	a large, bowl-shaped hole in the ground
dormant (*adjective*)	temporarily inactive
emits (*verb*)	produces or releases something
eruption (*noun*)	a loud, fiery explosion
evacuated (*verb*)	to be helped to leave a dangerous area
hazardous (*adjective*)	dangerous
mainland (*noun*)	the main mass of a continent or country, rather than its islands
plateau (*noun*)	a high, flat region
radar (*noun*)	a system for detecting objects by bouncing radio waves off them
radiating (*verb*)	being emitted in rays or waves
remote (*adjective*)	far away from large towns and cities
seismic (*adjective*)	relating to vibrations in Earth's crust
tectonic plates (*noun*)	the huge plates of solid rock that make up Earth's outer layer
thermal (*adjective*)	relating to heat
toxic (*adjective*)	poisonous
vent (*noun*)	an opening into an enclosed space, which gas or liquid can pass through

Index